The fire was dancing, the candles aglow—
So toasty inside, as the air filled with snow.
The wind whistled low while the mistletoe waited
For dear friends—and Christmas to be celebrated!

When out on the lawn there arose such a clatter,
Mickey sprang from his chair to see what was the matter.
Away to the door Mickey flew in a flash.
Had Goofy arrived with his usual CRASH?

Then what to his wondering eyes should appear
But a jingle-bell sleigh—were those really reindeer?
And a little old driver so cheerful and bright,
Could this be Uncle Scrooge? Yes, it was! What a sight!

With arms full of presents all ribboned and wrapped,
Out jumped a whole crew, as Scrooge called and he clapped:
"Out, Daisy! Out, Huey and Dewey and Louie!
Out, Donald! (And, Donald. . . on Christmas—no '*Phooey*'!)"

Then into the house with their bundles they bounded,
     While Christmassy meetings and greetings were sounded.
"Merry Christmas to you!" Mickey sang out with cheer.
     "We'll have a big dinner when everyone's here!"

Grandma Duck came a-calling a-hauling surprises:
Ornaments, tinsel, and Christmas tree prizes!
"Yoo-hoo!" called out Minnie. "May we join the fun?"
And Morty and Ferdie showed up on the run.

"Hiya, pal!" came a voice from a Pluto-led sleigh.
"It's Goofy!" cried Huey. "Grab snowballs! Let's play!"

As Donald and Daisy were trimming the tree,
　　Uncle Scrooge sorted presents. "Ah! Here's one for me!
Here's Donald's and Daisy's and Huey's and Dewey's,
　　There's Ferdie's and Morty's and Minnie's and Louie's,

And Grandma's and Goofy's and Mickey's—oh, dear!
    And Pluto's? Where's Pluto's? I can't find one here!"
Just then, "Time for dinner!" rang out through the house.
    Every creature was stirring—each dog, duck, and mouse!

Pass the turkey and stuffing and cranberries, please!
Mashed potatoes and gravy and carrots and peas!
More biscuits and butter, a thick slice of ham!
Pickles and applesauce. I'll take a yam!

Whose turn for the turnips? Here's corn on the cob!
The salt, if you please, and I'll take some eggnog.
Seconds for anyone? Now, don't be shy.
Did you get enough food?. . .

Did you save room for pie?
Cherry pie, berry pie, pumpkin pie, peach.
À la mode, Cheddar cheese, or a little of each?

When they'd filled themselves up from their heads
to their shoeses,
They all settled down for some short winter snoozes.
Each found a spot and soon dozed in their beds...

hile visions of Christmas
treats danced in their heads.

The wind gently blew; the snow danced and swirled.
Outside it was peaceful—a moonlit white world.
Then from out of the sky flew a wonderful sight:
It was jolly St. Nick on his Christmas Eve flight!

St. Nick crossed the roof with a leap and a bound,
  And sprang to the chimney, not making a sound.
On the hearth down below, Pluto thought, *What is this?*
  As a clump of wet snow doused the fire with a hiss.
Then all of a sudden, a man all in red
  Plopped right down that chimney…

. . . and patted his head!
This jolly old elf sat himself on his sack.
He scratched Pluto's ear. He patted his back.
"Merry Christmas!" he said, giving Pluto a hug.
Then he left that big sack on the living room rug.

And laying a finger aside of his nose,
And giving a nod—up the chimney he rose.
He called out to Pluto, "I'll see you next year!"
"Arf! Arf!" answered Pluto with tail-wagging cheer.

The clock chimed at midnight, and on the last stroke. . .
  "It's Christmas!" yawned Grandma.
Those nappers awoke!
    "Let's open the presents!" the kids called with glee.
"What's this?" Mickey asked. "There's a sack by the tree."

The tag read: "For Pluto, from your pal, St. Nick."
　　Mickey tugged on the string and it sprang open quick.
Here were big bones and long bones—why, bones of all sizes!
　　Dog chews and squeak toys—all sorts of surprises!

Said Mickey, "St. Nick must have come while we napped,
And he left Pluto's present for me to unwrap!
Now we all have our gifts, so let's give a big cheer!"